Alfred Zector,
BOOK COLLECTOR

For John, for everything
—K.D.

For Marijac
—M.P.

Alfred Zector, Book Collector
Text copyright © 2010 by Kelly DiPucchio
Illustrations copyright © 2010 by Macky Pamintuan

Manufactured in China.

Library of Congress Cataloging-in-Publication Data
DiPucchio, Kelly S.
    Alfred Zector, book collector / by Kelly DiPucchio ; illustrated by Macky
Pamintuan. — 1st ed.
        p.   cm.
    Summary: Alfred so loves books that he spends much of his life collecting
every one in his town, and when his collection is complete he sets out to read each
tome, while the lives of the townspeople grow dull and dreary.
    ISBN 978-0-06-000581-8 (trade bdg.) — ISBN 978-0-06-000582-5 (lib. bdg.)
    [1. Stories in rhyme.   2. Books and reading—Fiction.   3. Collectors and
collecting—Fiction.]   I. Pamintuan, Macky, ill.   II. Title.
PZ8.3.D5998Alf   2010   2008051771
[E]—dc22   CIP
                                                                      AC

Typography by Jeanne L. Hogle
10   11   12   13   14   S C P   10   9   8   7   6   5   4   3   2   1
❖
First Edition

Alfred Zector, BOOK COLLECTOR

by Kelly DiPucchio
illustrated by Macky Pamintuan

HARPER

An Imprint of HarperCollinsPublishers

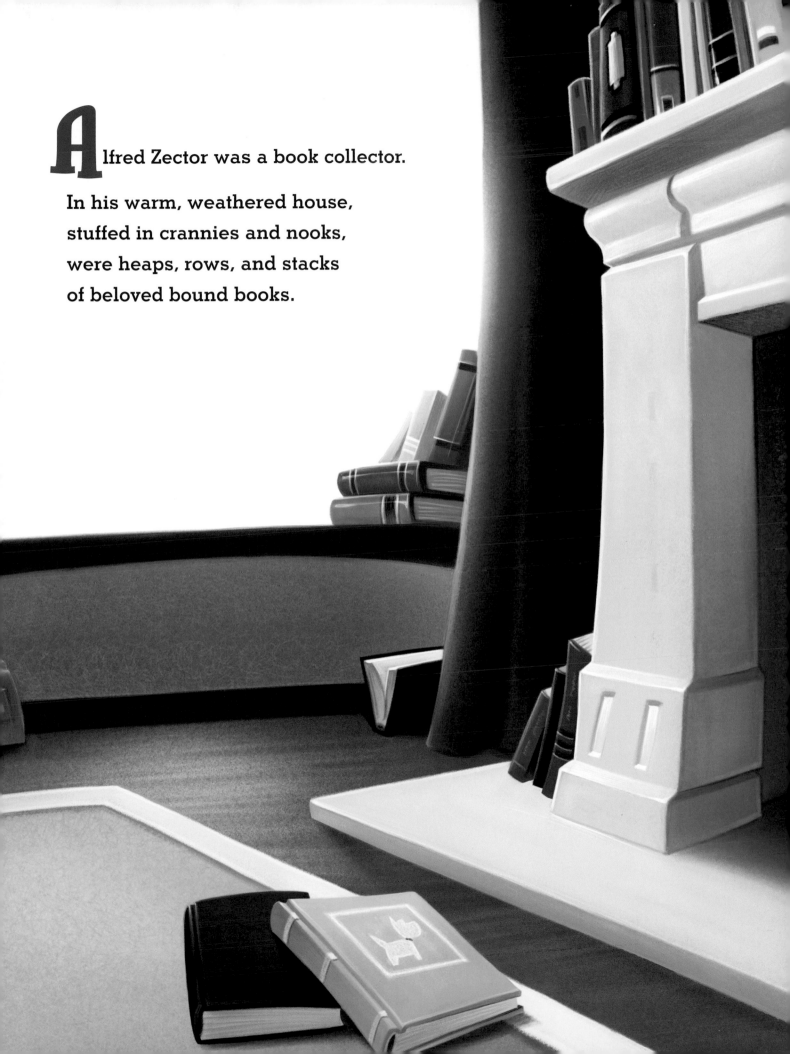

Alfred Zector was a book collector.

In his warm, weathered house,
stuffed in crannies and nooks,
were heaps, rows, and stacks
of beloved bound books.

As a child, young Alfred
just longed to belong.
But each time he tried
something always went wrong.

He was lonely and shy,
this bright, dreamy boy,
'til the day he discovered
that books brought him joy.

Time flew and stacks grew,
every shelf overflowing.
As Alfred got older,
his collection kept **GROWING!**

Alfred's cabinets were crammed
with novels, not dishes.

The aquarium housed . . .
The Encyclopedia of Fishes.

He thought he'd be happy
after only one more.
But that led to two books,
then three books,
then *four*!

Alfred inspected
the stacks tipping tall.
"Not enough," he decided.
"I must have them ALL!"

His home on the hill
was soon stretched at the seams,
but Alfred was close,
oh, so close,
to his dreams!

He scoured the city
on foot and on fours.
He overturned rocks
and he knocked on front doors.

At long last,
the end of his searching drew near.
His fingers, they trembled.
His eye held a tear.

The very last book
was owned by a tyke.
"I'll trade you that book for this shiny red bike."

The town was now emptied
of books big and small.
Alfred Zector, book collector,
had collected them all!

He carried in candles
and food by the load.
Then he locked the door shut
on his book-filled abode.

sLAM!

Alfred *should* have been happy.
His dream had come true!
But something was missing.
"*Now* what do I do?"

Tick.   Tick.

Tick . . .

. . . tocked the clock on the wall.
"Well, of course!" Alfred said.
"I must *read* them ALL!"

Days became weeks
and months became years.
Alfred read everything
from Seuss . . .
. . . to Shakespeare.

Meanwhile . . .

. . . life for the people
without books had become
quite dullish, plain dreary,
and wholly humdrum.

Conversations were bland,
and bedtime a bore.
There were children
who'd never been read to before!

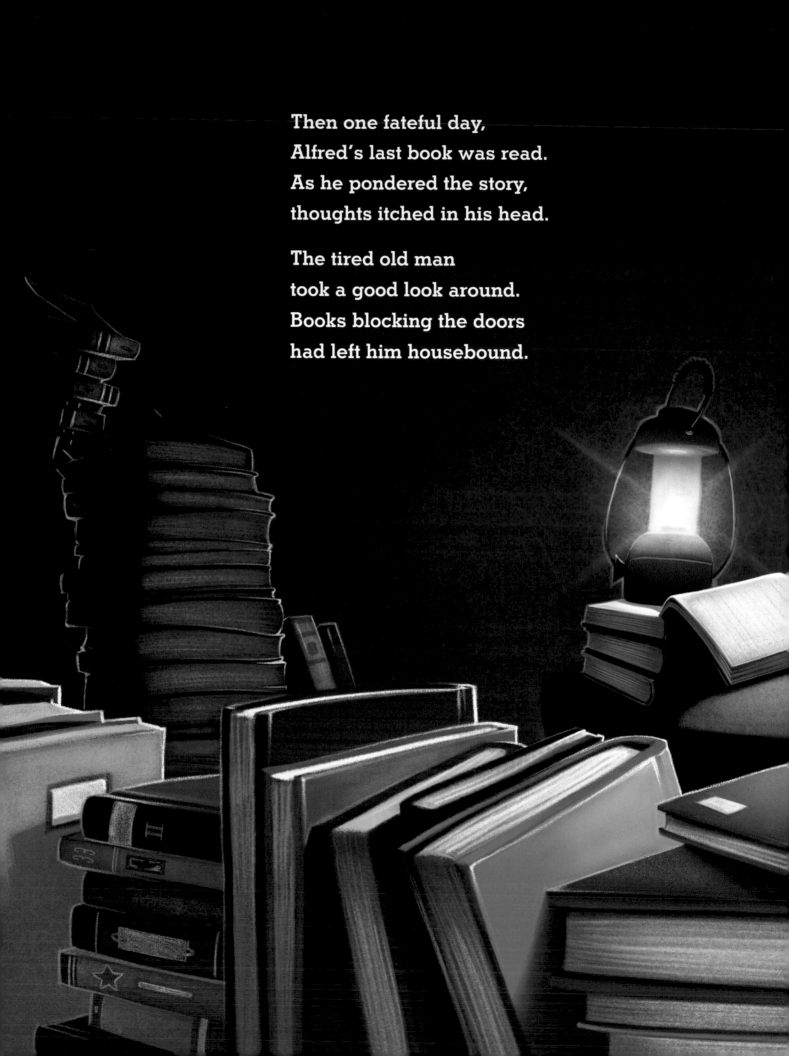

Then one fateful day,
Alfred's last book was read.
As he pondered the story,
thoughts itched in his head.

The tired old man
took a good look around.
Books blocking the doors
had left him housebound.

The joy he'd once felt
was replaced by sheer *doom*.
The books that he loved
had created his tomb!

Alfred felt smothered.
"Now what?" he cried.
"Something's *still* missing!
What *is* it?" he sighed.

Alfred shuffled and shimmied
up the tall chimney stack.
He emerged out the top
of his weed-woven shack.

There on the roof
he sat very still . . .
'til a rusty red bike
rattled over the hill.

Now, all of that reading
made Alfred quite smart.
Thoughts sprang from his head
and they spread to his heart!

"I FIGURED IT OUT!"
Alfred called from the thatch.
"Excuse me, young man!
Here's a gift for you! *Catch."*

Alfred felt giddy
and free as a bird.
"There's more where that came from!
Go spread the word."

Alfred gave books
to the young and the old.
He laughed and he smiled
as stories were told.

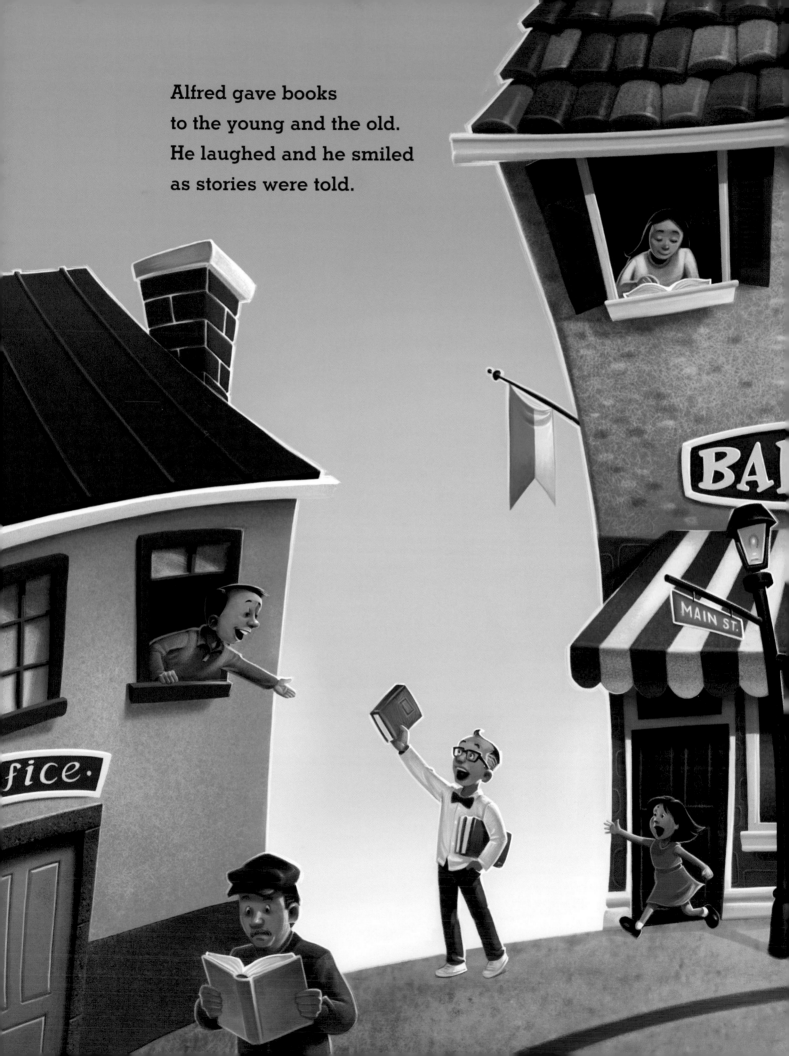

Once again,
folks were reading
all over the town . . .
in bakeries,
on buses,
in trees,
upside down!

Surrounded by friends,
Alfred Zector declared,
"The best kinds of books
are the books that are shared."